Sister Magic

The Trouble with Violet

BY **ANNE MAZER**

ILLUSTRATIONS BY BILL BROWN

SCHOLASTIC INC.

New York Toronto London Auckland Sydney
Mexico City New Delhi Hong Kong Buenos Aires

Many thanks to all who contributed their magic:
Craig Walker, Kate Egan, Elaine Markson,
Gary Johnson, Catherine Daly, Anica Rissi,
Mariah Balaban, and Michele Mortlock

ISBN-13: 978-0-439-87246-1
ISBN-10: 0-439-87246-4

12 11 10 9 8 7 6 5 4 3 2   7 8 9 10 11 12/0

Printed in the U.S.A.   40
First printing, July 2007

Chapter One

Mabel and Violet were as different as two sisters could be.

They didn't look alike. They didn't think alike. They didn't play alike. They didn't act alike.

Sometimes they didn't even like each other.

One day at the end of the summer, a package arrived. It was addressed to both Mabel and Violet.

The package was wrapped in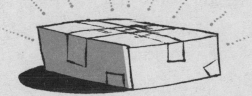

shiny white paper and sealed with packing tape. It was square and heavy. Mabel didn't recognize the return address.

She brought it inside.

Violet jumped up and down with excitement. "What is it? Who sent it?"

"I don't have X-ray vision," Mabel said a little crossly. "Calm down, Violet."

But she also wondered who had sent it and why. It wasn't anyone's birthday. It wasn't even a holiday. Was it something they needed for school?

She opened the package.

It was an old-fashioned fairy-tale book. On the inside of the cover was an inscription in glittery silver ink. It said: "To my dear nieces, Mabel and Violet."

It was signed: "Uncle Vartan."

Mabel and Violet received cards and birthday presents from Uncle Vartan every year. But they had never met him in person. Mabel imagined him as a thin old man with a long white beard who drank tea and kept cats.

Mabel examined the book. It had thick creamy pages, fancy lettering, and pictures you could practically walk into. It even had its own bookmark in deep crimson velvet.

It was the most beautiful book that Mabel had ever seen.

"My turn!" Violet cried. "Let me see it!"

Mabel looked at Violet. She had jam on her face. She had jam on her hands. She even had jam in her hair.

There was no way that Mabel was going to share this book with her.

Even though it was Violet's book, too.

Mabel took the book into her room.

Violet followed her. "Can I have the book now?" she asked.

"Not if you're going to ruin it."

"I *won't*." Violet reached for it with a sticky hand. "I'll take good care of it."

"The way you took care of my doll?" Mabel demanded.

Violet had given the doll a spiked haircut. She had colored its lips bright green for spring. She had written on the doll's arm and said it was a tattoo.

"I'll be very, very, *very* careful when I read the book," Violet said. "I promise!"

"Oh yeah?" Mabel said. Violet made promises all the time. She broke them whenever she felt like it.

"I'll even clean my hands first." Violet wiped her hands on the sides of her T-shirt, then rubbed at the dirt on her elbows. "See?"

"See *what*?" Mabel asked. She wrapped her arms around the book.

"Please, Mabel," Violet begged.

Mabel looked at Violet. Her little sister was way too immature to appreciate a book like this. What had Uncle Vartan been thinking?

"No," she said. "I won't give it to you."

Violet was mad. She ran to tell on Mabel. Their mother sent Mabel to her room.

Mabel had to stay there until she was ready to share the book with her grubby little sister.

That would be never.

Or at least until lunchtime.

Mabel took out a piece of paper and drew a neat line exactly down the middle. Then she began to write:

MABEL: FACTS	VIOLET: FACTS
eight years old	five years old
starting third grade	starting kindergarten
neat, combed, straight hair	tangled, snarly hair
round face, dark eyes	jam-smeared face
flossed, brushed teeth	what's a toothbrush?
very organized	a total slob
never forgets chores	what ARE chores?

Graphs, charts, and lists always calmed Mabel down. They reminded her of the way things were supposed to be: predictable and organized. Mabel liked results that she could see.

If only her little sister was as neat and orderly as a chart or graph. Mabel wished Violet was more like *her*.

Chapter Two

That afternoon, Mabel's friend Simone came over.

Simone was tall. She had long black hair, which she wore braided around her head.

Simone wore pointy blue glasses. She had a wide smile and slightly crooked teeth.

"Are you excited about kindergarten?" Simone asked Violet.

Violet nodded.

"You're going to love it!" Simone said. "My favorite part was reading."

"Reading." Violet suddenly looked nervous. She didn't know how to do that yet.

Mabel changed the subject. "Does anyone want to make necklaces?" she asked.

Simone crouched down to Violet's level. "Don't worry," she said. "You'll do fine, Violet. Who's your teacher?"

"Mr. Bland," Violet whispered.

"Beads, anyone?" Mabel repeated.

"Mr. Bland is so nice!" Simone said. "He never yells or anything like that."

Violet breathed a sigh of relief.

"I'm getting out the beads," Mabel said.

She brought her special bead box out to the dining room. She had organized the beads by size, color, and shape. All the colors of the rainbow, from blue-green to yellow-orange, sparkled in their drawers.

Mabel didn't usually let anyone else touch them.

She was very proud of herself for sharing.

The girls sat down. Mabel gave everyone a cord and a small container for their beads.

Outside, the sun was shining. It lit up the beads on the dining room table.

"Isn't this fun?" Mabel asked, picking up a blue bead. "I love to bead."

"I can't think of anything better to do on a warm, beautiful summer day," said Simone, stifling a yawn.

"Me, neither," Mabel said.

Simone began to sort through the beads. "You don't have enough square red ones," she said. "I want to make a necklace with them."

"Do we have to do this?" Violet said.

Mabel frowned. "Don't you want to wear your very own, handmade, unique necklace on the first day of school?"

"Not really," Violet said.

"Not even one with all your favorite colors?" Mabel continued.

"No." Violet pushed back her chair and stood up. "I want to play in the backyard. I'm going to run under the sprinkler."

Mabel looked at Simone. Her friend jumped to her feet to help out.

But Simone didn't say, "Please stay with us, Violet." Instead she said, "I'll turn on the sprinkler for you."

Mabel couldn't believe it.

"Do you want to come outside with us, Mabel?" Simone asked.

Mabel picked up a gold bead. "I think I'll finish my necklace."

I don't mind, Mabel told herself.

I don't mind sitting all alone.

She didn't mind hearing shrieks of laughter from the backyard.

She didn't mind that Simone had gone off with her little sister.

Beading was her *very* favorite activity.

She was going to make a necklace to wear on the first day of school. Her new teacher would be so impressed to learn that she had made it herself.

*   *   *

Mabel glanced out the window. The sun was shining. The sky was blue. It was hot and breezy outside.

And school wasn't starting for five more days.

She could finish the necklace anytime before then. She could even make a matching bracelet.

There was plenty of time.

But there might not be time to run under the sprinkler again.

Mabel had to admit that Violet sometimes had good ideas.

And sometimes she just had to go along with them.

Mabel put away the beads and her unfinished necklace, then hurried upstairs to change into a bathing suit.

When she came out of the house, the

sprinkler was casting jets of water over Violet and Simone. They were drenched and laughing.

"I'm here!" Mabel yelled. She ran to join them.

Chapter Three

It was Violet's bedtime. Mabel entered her room with Uncle Vartan's book under her arm.

"Are you ready, Violet?" she asked.

She winced as she looked at Violet's walls.

Each one was painted a different color: bright orange, pink, red, or turquoise. Violet's curtains were green. She had a polka-dotted bedspread.

It's all too much, Mabel thought. Violet's room gave her a headache.

Mabel's room was painted one color only: pale yellow. Her curtains were yellow.

Her bedspread was cream. Her furniture was white.

Mabel organized her clothes by color. Her books were alphabetized. Her toys were grouped in families.

She even had an empty shelf for the awards she was going to win this year.

Her first trophy might be the Good Sister Award. Mabel had offered to read Violet a chapter of Uncle Vartan's book every night before bed.

"But only if you stay very quiet," she told Violet. "And no touching the pages."

"How am I going to see the pictures?" Violet asked

"I'll show them to you."

"Can I look as much as I want?"

"Yes," Mabel promised. "As long as you don't touch the book."

"Reading to Violet at bedtime? That's my big girl!" their mother said when she heard.

She gave Mabel an extra scoop of ice cream for dessert.

And she gave her permission to stay up an extra half an hour that night.

Mabel felt a little guilty.

She wasn't really thinking about Violet. She was only thinking about how to keep Violet's careless, grubby fingers away from Uncle Vartan's book.

That night Mabel sat down on Violet's polka-dotted bed, opened the book, and began. "Once upon a —"

"What's that squiggly snake thing doing?" Violet interrupted.

"That's the letter S, Violet," Mabel said patiently.

"It hissed at me."

Mabel rolled her eyes. "Letters don't hiss."

"This one did," Violet insisted.

Mabel went on. ". . . time, there lived a young magician named Merriweather who lived in the kingdom of Morania . . ."

Violet waved at the picture of the young magician. "He said hello to me," she announced.

"*Shh*," Mabel said. ". . . with his mother, father, and three beautiful sisters —"

"His mother, father, two beautiful brothers, and one ugly sister," Violet corrected. "With three warts on her nose."

"That's not in the story!" Mabel said. She continued. ". . . in the town of Snowflower —"

"Snowfall," Violet interrupted again.

Mabel slammed the book shut. "Who's reading: you or me?"

"But, Mabel, I *know* —"

"You don't know anything!" Mabel cried. "You don't even know the alphabet!"

"I *do*." Violet counted on her fingers: "A, B, D, Q, X, C, L. Finish the story now, Mabel."

"If you don't interrupt again."

"But what if you get it wrong?"

"*I'm* the one who can read, not you!" Mabel said. "You don't *know* if I make a mistake!"

"Yes I do," Violet said stubbornly.

Mabel let out a long breath. This was harder than she thought it would be. "Please, Violet," she said.

Mabel suddenly had an idea. "In kindergarten, when the teacher reads a story, all the students have to listen quietly. Let's practice for school, okay?"

To her relief, Violet nodded. She picked up her stuffed monkey and put her thumb in her mouth.

"All right then," Mabel said. She opened the book. "We'll start over. Listen quietly. Just like kindergarten, okay?"

The book was exciting. It was full of magicians, enchanted forests, and mysterious strangers with long white beards.

Mabel usually liked a different kind of book. She liked books about pioneer girls, or girls who trained horses, or starred in the school play.

She could relate to stories like that. They were real.

But Uncle Vartan's storybook was good, too. Even if everything in it was made up.

One of these days, even Violet would understand what was real and what wasn't. For example, the letter S never hissed at anyone. And magicians in books didn't wave hello to little girls.

Violet loved the book. She listened intently.

By the end of the chapter, Violet's eyes were closing. When Mabel tiptoed to the door and shut off the light, her sister was sound asleep.

Chapter Four

Mabel felt extremely proud of herself.

She had taught Violet good listening skills for kindergarten. She had put her sister to sleep. She had protected Uncle Vartan's book from stains, bent pages, and careless handling. She had protected it from *Violet*.

Now, back in her room, she took out a piece of paper. It was time to make a couple of lists.

THINGS TO DO BEFORE SCHOOL STARTS:

1. Finish beaded necklace and make matching bracelet.
2. Write down all books read over summer.
3. Teach Violet everything she needs to know for kindergarten.
4. Organize desk drawers and closet.

It was a lot, but Mabel could handle it. She chewed thoughtfully on the end of her pen. Then she began to write the next one.

THINGS FOR MOM TO DO BEFORE SCHOOL STARTS:

1. Take Violet and me shoe shopping.
2. Buy us school supplies: ruler, pencils, crayons, tissues, backpack, etc.
3. Get Violet new school clothes.

REMIND MOM:

1. *To make sure Violet gets MATCHING clothes.*
2. *That I'm working at Dad's store tomorrow afternoon.*
3. *That I'll get all MY new school clothes at his store, like I always do.*

Mabel rercad the lists. She frowned. There were three items on her mother's list and four items on her list. That added up to two to-do lists, three reminders, and five days before the start of school.

She had better get her mother organized right away.

And while she was at it, she would tell her mother that Violet was asleep. It wasn't always so easy to settle Violet down.

Her mother was downstairs in the sun-room. She was on the phone with her older sister, Dolores.

Aunt Dolores didn't have any children of

her own, so Mabel had gotten all of the attention. That is, until Violet came along.

Now Violet got most of the hugs and kisses.

It was like that with little sisters and brothers. Mabel tried not to mind too much.

Her mother was deep in conversation. She didn't notice Mabel coming into the sunroom.

"Vartan sent them a book of fairy tales," she was saying. "Mabel is upstairs reading it to Violet."

Mabel stopped and waited.

Now came the part where her mother said, "I can always count on Mabel," or "Mabel is such a big help."

Instead, her mother lowered her voice. "I *think* it's okay," she said. "I know she's getting to that age where . . ."

Where what? Mabel leaned forward to catch her words.

"It could be a big problem for our family," her mother went on. She was silent a moment, listening to Dolores's response.

Me? A problem? Mabel couldn't believe what she was hearing.

Her mother said, "I don't want anyone to know."

What in the world were they talking about? Mabel crept closer. A floorboard squeaked.

Her mother turned around. "Mabel!"

She looked worried. "How long have you been here?"

"Uh, not long," she stammered.

"You know it's wrong to eavesdrop."

"I wasn't," Mabel protested. "I put Violet to sleep all by myself. And I wanted to ask you about back-to-school shopping."

"Not now, honey. I'm talking to Aunt Dolores."

"About what?"

Her mother waved her away. "It's a grown-up thing."

She didn't say "thank you." Mabel let the door bang behind her.

Then she stomped upstairs to her room and lay down on the bed to think.

"She's getting to that age . . ." her mother had said.

What age was that?

"Am I old enough to stay up until ten?" Mabel asked herself out loud. "Do more chores? Bike to the park by myself? Not worry about Violet anymore?"

But why would any of those be a problem for the family?

The more Mabel thought about it, the less she understood.

Chapter Five

The saleswoman at the shoe store knelt down to tie the laces on Violet's new sneakers. "How do they feel?"

Violet looked down at the tangerine high-tops. "They feel . . . *orange*," she said. "Like soda for my feet."

The saleswoman glanced at Mabel's mother. "She's adorable," she said.

Mabel sighed. Her little sister was always adorable. Except when she was embarrassing.

Violet bounced out of her seat. She skipped around the store, glanced at her tangerine feet in the mirror, and then returned to her mother and sister.

"I want them," she said.

Her mother nodded.

"Tangerine high-tops?" Mabel said. *No one* in school wore sneakers like that. "Are you sure?"

And besides, her little sister already had aqua pants, pink socks, and yellow and lime green T-shirts. She was going to look like a walking box of crayons.

Not to mention the long laces.

"What about Velcro sneakers?" Mabel suggested.

"I know how to tie laces," Violet said.

"No you don't," Mabel said.

"Yes I *do*," Violet said.

Their mother frowned at Mabel. "Violet can handle lace-ups. Be positive, Mabel."

Why was it Mabel's fault? She was only telling the truth. Her mother wasn't going to be there to tie Violet's laces when they came undone on the way to school.

Mabel slumped back in her chair. Her mother asked the saleswoman how much the high-top sneakers cost.

"They're on special today. Fifty percent off," she said.

Great, Mabel thought. Probably no one else wants to buy them.

"We don't have them in Velcro," the saleswoman added.

"Never mind that," her mother said. "We'll take them. And now Mabel needs sneakers, too."

Usually this was Mabel's favorite part of back-to-school shopping. She loved getting new shoes.

"Do you want tangerine high-tops?" the saleswoman asked. "To match your little sister's?"

Mabel couldn't think of anything she wanted less. *"No!"* she practically shouted, and then, remembering her manners, added, "thank you."

"How about this brand-new rose and turquoise model? It's very popular with girls your age."

"I want something that will coordinate with all my outfits," Mabel said. "Something classic."

The saleswoman brought out a stack of boxes. She opened the first one and brought out a pair of beige tennis sneakers.

They were too plain, but Mabel decided to try them on anyway.

"I can do it myself," Mabel said as the saleswoman knelt down to help her tie them.

Mabel began to tighten the laces. "You see, Violet, *this* is how you tie a shoe. First, you tighten the laces, then you pull them at the top . . ."

"I *know*," Violet said. She scowled at Mabel.

"You do *not* know," Mabel said, standing up. "And I don't want to do it for you every single morning."

Mabel looked down at her feet. She heard a faint *pop*. The laces had come undone.

"How did that happen?" Mabel said. She sat down again, yanked the shoelaces as tight as she could, and then double-knotted them.

"This way, they *never* come untied," she told her little sister. "Got it?"

She wiggled her toes. The laces popped open again.

"Mabel can't tie her shoes!" Violet crowed. *"Mabel can't tie her shoes!"*

"That's *not* true!" Mabel's face turned bright red.

She tried again. But the laces wouldn't stay tied. "There's something wrong with these sneakers. Let me try another pair."

The saleswoman handed Mabel a pair of white sneakers. They came unlaced, too.

"Are you sure you're tying them right, Mabel?" her mother asked.

"Yes!" Mabel jammed a third pair of sneakers on her feet. This time, she didn't tie them. As she stood up, the long laces trailed on the floor.

"Don't trip, Mabel," Violet warned her.

Mabel stepped in front of a mirror. She checked out the sneakers.

Okay, they were untied. They were loose. They didn't fit the way they would if she had tied them.

But they seemed comfortable enough. They were navy blue, just the right color to go with all of her outfits.

Something was strange, though. When Mabel looked in the mirror, her reflection kept fading in and out.

There she was. Now she was gone.

It was like bad TV reception.

Except she wasn't a television set.

Mabel pinched her arm and then her cheek, to make sure she was really there. Yes, she was.

She blinked. Her feet were gone. She blinked again. They were back.

Mabel rubbed her eyes. Maybe she needed glasses, like Simone?

Last week, the eye doctor had told her mother that Mabel had perfect vision.

Was it the mirror? All of its reflections — the store, the shoes, the customers — looked normal.

Except for Mabel. Her reflection kept going in and out of focus.

Oh no, Mabel thought.

She suddenly knew what her mother might be worrying about. It would certainly be a "big problem for the family."

Mabel wondered if she was going crazy.

Chapter Six

The next afternoon Mabel wheeled a basket of clothing around her father's store, Clothes to You.

She stopped at a display of fall coats. Mabel took a corduroy jacket from the basket and hung it up neatly on its rack.

"Helping out today?" a customer asked.

Mabel nodded proudly. She wheeled the basket to another rack.

Today was a special day.

Her father had hired her to work in the store. He always needed lots of extra help the week before school started.

"I need dependable hands," he said,

putting his arm around Mabel. "I can always count on my number one helper."

Clothes to You sold clothing for children and adults. It also sold snow boots, hats, and some toys.

The store had six fitting rooms.

Mabel's job was to hang up the clothes left inside them.

She put the clothes on hangers, straightened them, and returned them to the correct rack.

She made sure that all the sizes and colors were in order.

Sometimes her father even let her wait on customers.

Mabel loved working at her father's store.

Violet wanted to work at the store, too.

"I'm sorry, we're very busy today, Violet," her father said. "We can't spare anyone to keep an eye on you."

"Wait until you're a big girl, and going

into third grade like Mabel," her mother promised.

Mabel and her father exchanged a glance. *Maybe* Violet would work at the store in a few years. And maybe not.

When Violet visited the store, she hid in the racks. She took sales stickers off the tags. She tried on men's socks and boy's bathing suits.

Someone had to watch her all the time. No one ever had to watch Mabel.

Today was special for another reason, too.

When Mabel was done working, she would pick out her new clothes for the school year.

While she worked, Mabel made a list:

WARDROBE (she named it in her head)
Plaid kilt and matching sweater
Long-sleeved button-down shirts,
    white, rose, and pale yellow
Navy and khaki pants
Dark red wool jacket
Headbands
Kneesocks
A set of days-of-the-week underwear

Mabel had always wished for a school uniform. But picking out her own uniform from her father's store was almost better.

It made her father happy — and it made Mabel happy, too, because she could get exactly what she wanted.

Mabel's father always made her feel special. And he seemed to understand how difficult it was to have a younger sister like Violet, even though he never said an unkind word about either of the girls.

Mabel loved it when he walked her to school. They talked about everything: school, homework, things that made them laugh, and their favorite movie scenes.

Thinking about it, she smiled.

As she passed a floor-length mirror, Mabel caught sight of herself. She stopped and waited for her reflection to fade in and out, the way it had yesterday.

It didn't.

She glanced in another mirror, and another. Still there.

Thank goodness!

Mabel replaced a pair of sweatpants on the rack. She straightened a row of jogging shorts and folded a sweatshirt.

She wondered if she had imagined it all.

But that wasn't good, either. She still might be losing her mind. Maybe that's why she hadn't been able to tie her sneakers.

Her father walked down the aisle.

"Dad, am I, uh, at the age where I might, um, cause a big problem for the family?" Mabel said, repeating her mother's words.

He looked startled by her question. "Of course not, pumpkin. You've never caused us *any* problems."

"Well, are there, like, crazy people in our family?" Mabel continued.

Her father thought for a moment. "There are some people I'd definitely call eccentric," he said. "Or maybe a little odd. But not crazy."

"What about kids?"

"No one that I know of." Her father picked up a T-shirt that had fallen on the floor. "Are you thinking of anyone in particular?"

"Um, well . . . me," Mabel blurted.

"*You?* Crazy?" her father said in astonishment. "Now *that's* crazy. You're one of the most sensible kids I know."

"You're sure?"

"I'm one hundred percent sure."

Mabel breathed a sigh of relief. "Thanks, Dad. I won't worry about it anymore."

"That's my girl," her father said proudly.

Chapter Seven

"You were a great help today," Mabel's father said. He pulled into the driveway and put the car into park. Then he handed her three folded five-dollar bills. "You've earned every cent of this."

Mabel beamed with pride. Tomorrow she would go to the bank and deposit the money in her savings account.

"Help your mother out, okay, pumpkin? I'm going back to the store for another hour or two."

"Okay, Dad." Mabel leaned over to kiss him on the cheek. She jumped out of the car, waved, and ran up the stairs.

✳   ✳   ✳

Mabel opened the door of her house and found her mother in the entry hall on the floor. She was surrounded by the contents of her purse.

Lipsticks, pens, cards, books, and her weekly organizer were jumbled together in a heap.

"It's not here," Mabel's mother said over and over. *"It's not here."*

"Mom?" Mabel said. "What's wrong?"

Her mother looked up. "I lost my wallet!" she said. "I can't find it anywhere. I'm going to have to cancel our credit cards." She looked ready to cry.

Mabel took a deep breath. She was here. She was ready. She knew just what to do.

She pulled out a notepad from her pocket. "Let's get organized, Mom. Let's make a list of all the places you might have left it."

Her mother shot her a grateful look. "Thank you, Mabel. What would I do without you?"

44

"It's nothing," Mabel said with a modest shrug.

Violet suddenly appeared in the hallway. She had paint stains on her clothes. Her feet were bare and dirty. A brush stiff with dried paint poked out of her pocket.

"What's all that stuff on the floor?" she asked.

"I'm looking for a missing wallet," her mother explained.

"Oh," Violet said, wandering out of the room again.

Mabel uncapped her pen. She was ready to get down to business. "Mom? Let's retrace your steps. Where did you last see your wallet? What were you doing?"

"I was in the hallway," her mother said. "I was taking a pink lipstick out of my purse . . ."

"Did you search your purse?" Mabel asked.

"Three times."

"Desk drawers? Tables? Grocery bags?"

"I've looked in all of those places," her mother said.

Violet wandered back in. "Did you find it?"

"Not yet," her mother said.

"I'll help," Violet offered. She plunked herself down on the floor, crossed her legs, and closed her eyes.

Mabel tried to ignore her.

"Your wallet is someplace very, very cold," Violet announced with a shiver. "I see ice cubes."

"Ice cubes?" her mother repeated. "I don't think so, honey."

"And frost everywhere," Violet added.

Mabel coughed. Why had *she* worried about going crazy? If anyone was crazy in this family, it was Violet.

"Please don't interrupt again," she said to her. "We're doing important work here."

"It's in the freezer," Violet concluded. She opened her eyes, got up, and left the room.

Thank goodness, Mabel thought.

"Where else might you have left your wallet?" she asked her mother. Even Violet's nuttiest ideas couldn't throw her investigation off course.

I'd make a good private detective, Mabel said to herself.

Or maybe a television interviewer.

"Um, in the living room? I looked under

the couch cushions," her mother said. "Really, Mabel, I've looked *everywhere*."

Mabel jumped up. She searched behind the television and under the rocking chair. She checked all the windowsills and ran a hand over the top of the bookshelf. She pulled books out from the bookcase.

Nothing.

When she returned, her mother was emptying coat pockets.

"I have a package of gum, six dollars in spare change, some crumpled tissues, and a lost library card here," she said sadly. "But no wallet."

"Mom, we'll search every inch of this house until we find it," Mabel promised in her best professional manner.

Violet appeared again.

"What *now*?" Mabel said.

"I found it." Violet held up the wallet.

It was frosty. The ice crystals on the clasp were starting to melt. There was a steady drip from the wallet to the floor.

Her mother practi-
cally exploded with
joy. "Violet! You angel!
You dream child! You
five-year-old wonder!
You found it!"

She wiped a bit of frost from the wallet.
"They must have frozen my account," she
joked.

"Mom," Mabel said. She couldn't believe
this. "*How* did your wallet get in the *freezer*?"

"Um, maybe I threw it in with the frozen
peas?" her mother said. "Or with the fish
sticks?"

"And you didn't notice?" Mabel said in
disbelief. The *really* unbelievable thing was
that Violet had known the wallet was there.
And all she had done was sit down and
close her eyes.

Or maybe she had put it in the freezer
herself? No, even Violet wouldn't do that.
And besides, it took time to grow all those
ice crystals.

"Oh, who cares how the wallet got there?" her mother cried. "All that matters is that I have it back."

She turned to Violet again. "Violet, you're the absolute best. You saved my life. I don't know how you did it."

"Neither do I," Mabel muttered. None of this made any sense to her at all. Her *sister* didn't make any sense to her at all.

It was Violet's turn to beam with pride. "I'm a big girl," she said.

"You sure are," her mother said. "Thank you a thousand times over."

Violet sure got lucky, Mabel thought. *But what about* me*? Don't I get any thanks?*

Chapter Eight

After all the excitement about the wallet, Mabel's mother had decided that it was a good night to order in.

The pizza had just arrived. Everyone was starving.

Mabel's father opened the first box.

"Sandra?" he said to his wife with a puzzled frown. "What did you order?"

"Two large plain pizzas," she said. "Why?"

"They gave us pepperoni."

"Oh dear," she said. "They probably mixed up the orders. Do you want me to call and ask for a replacement?"

"I can't wait for it to come," he said. "It

was so busy at the store today that I skipped lunch. Right now I'd eat anything."

He picked up a slice of pizza and put it on a plate. "Who wants the first piece?"

"Me!" Violet said. "I *love* pepperoni pizza!"

"It's your lucky day, Violet," her father said, handing her a big slice.

"It's not *my* lucky day," Mabel grumbled. She didn't like anything on her pizza, ever.

Her father passed her a small slice. Frowning, Mabel picked off the pepperoni. She took a bite. *Ewww*. She could still taste the pepperoni.

Why did they have to get someone else's order? And why today of all days?

First the wallet in the freezer, and now a mixed-up pizza order. Yesterday crazy shoelaces and a vanishing reflection.

A lot of odd things had happened over the last couple of days.

But what did it mean?

Like her father said, it was probably pure coincidence. They were having a run of bad luck.

Except for Violet, of course. That's what was bothering Mabel the most.

Mabel's mother poured some cranberry juice in a glass. "Simone came over today," she said. "She was looking for you, Mabel."

"Did you tell her I was at work?" Mabel felt very grown up.

"Yes, I did," her mother said. "She was sorry to miss you. Luckily, Violet was here."

"Simone and I went to the park," Violet said. She passed her plate for another slice of pizza. "We played soccer."

"You and Simone?"

Violet nodded. "We had fun."

But Simone is my *friend,* Mabel thought. She hoped Simone was still her friend after a few hours with Violet. She hoped that Violet didn't do anything embarrassing.

Like talk to the soccer ball. Or, even worse, pretend that it was talking to her. Or invent her own rules for the game. You never knew what Violet would do.

After that, everyone was quiet. They ate pizza. The clock ticked on the wall. A warm breeze fluttered the curtains.

Then the doorbell rang loudly and broke the silence.

"What now?" their father said.

It rang again. No one moved.

"I'll get it!" Violet slid out of her seat.

"Ask to be excused, Violet!" Mabel called after her. Someone had to remind her of her table manners.

When Violet returned a few minutes later, she was holding the hand of a stranger.

Mabel wished that her little sister wouldn't hold strangers' hands. It just wasn't right. Especially strangers like this one.

He looked familiar, although Mabel had never seen him before. He wore a blue

seersucker suit and a white shirt with silver cuff links. He carried a large leather satchel. There were rings on his fingers. His eyes were pale blue like the sky on a windy day.

"Hello, Sandra," the stranger said. "Hello, Arthur."

How did he know her parents' names?

"Aren't you glad to see me?" he asked. "Your very own baby brother?"

Baby brother? *Whose* baby brother?

Not Mabel's. Not her father's — he was an only child. Her mother's? Her mother had a sister, Aunt Dolores. She couldn't have a brother, too, or Mabel would have known about him.

Wouldn't Mabel have known about him?

"Vartan," her mother croaked. She was almost too shocked to speak.

"Uncle Vartan? This is Uncle *Vartan*?" Mabel said.

Mabel had always thought that Uncle Vartan was her great-uncle.

She never imagined him as younger than her father. She never imagined him in a seersucker suit with silver cuff links.

She never imagined he would show up on their doorstep, unannounced.

And she especially never imagined him as a baby brother. Why hadn't she known this before now?

Chapter Nine

Her father was the first to recover his wits. "Vartan!" he cried, pumping his hand. "Welcome! It's been over ten years, hasn't it? We last saw you at our wedding. And now we have two beautiful daughters."

Uncle Vartan turned to Mabel first.

"So this is Mabel," he said. "A loyal, reliable friend. A girl with an excellent head on her shoulders."

"You've got that right," her father agreed.

Mabel's head spun with the compliments. How did Uncle Vartan know these things about her?

Uncle Vartan put his arm around Violet.

"And this must be wild, wonderful Violet. We've already met."

"Lots of times," Violet said. "We went on a picnic. Uncle Vartan and I climbed trees together. I flew a kite with him."

Mabel shook her head. When would Violet start telling the truth?

"Sit down, Vartan," their father said. "Have some pepperoni pizza." He pointed to the second box. "We have plenty; Sandra ordered extra tonight."

Uncle Vartan pulled up a chair. He put a large white cloth napkin on his lap. Then he adjusted his silver cuff links.

"Pepperoni? My favorite," he said. The lights flickered. A wind gusted through the room.

Mabel's mother knocked over her glass of cranberry juice. Quickly, she grabbed a napkin to wipe up the spill.

"What brings you here?" their father asked.

"Just passing through." Vartan poured himself a drink.

"'Just passing through' after ten years?" Their mother spoke for the first time.

Vartan nodded.

"You're welcome to stay for as long as you like," their father said. "Relax, take in the sights, spend time with the girls. . . ."

"When are you leaving?" their mother asked Vartan.

"I haven't decided yet." Vartan winked at the girls. "Don't worry, Sandra, I won't be a burden on you."

"That's not what I'm worried about," their mother said, "and you know it."

There was a slight tension in the air.

Mabel caught Violet's eye.

"We love the book you sent us, Uncle Vartan," Mabel said. "I'm reading it to Violet a little bit every night."

"Good, good," Uncle Vartan said. "I'd like to read you girls a few chapters sometime myself." With one smooth

motion, he slid the entire pizza onto his plate.

The girls stared.

"Are you going to eat the whole thing?" Violet asked.

"I am."

"Same appetite as always, Vartan." Their mother quickly drank a glass of water. "Good thing we've already eaten."

"I'm a growing man," he said, winking again at the girls.

Mabel gawked. She knew it was rude, but she had never met anyone like Uncle Vartan. She just couldn't help herself.

Chapter Ten

Mabel woke up early the next morning. She tiptoed into Violet's room.

Violet's orange, pink, red, and turquoise walls seemed even brighter in the morning sun. The green curtains fluttered in the breeze.

Violet was sound asleep.

Mabel sat down on the edge of Violet's polka-dotted bed and waited for her to wake up.

Mabel thought about Uncle Vartan. There was something about him that she couldn't put her finger on.

Well, for one thing, she had never seen

his picture. She suddenly realized how strange that was. Had he been erased out of the family album? And why?

Violet turned over in bed and opened her eyes.

"Hey," Mabel said.

Violet stretched and yawned. "Is Uncle Vartan up?"

Mabel shook her head. "Probably not."

Was Violet curious, too?

"Hey, Violet, did you know that Mom had a little brother?" Mabel asked. "I mean, did you know before last night?"

"Uh-uh."

"Me, neither," Mabel said. "I thought he was a great-uncle or something."

"He sends us presents," Violet said.

"But we never write him thank-you notes." Mabel frowned at her little sister. "Mom *always* makes us write them to everyone else," she said. "Isn't that a little odd?"

Violet climbed out of bed and put on a

T-shirt and shorts. "I'm going to see him now," she announced.

"Um, not a good idea," Mabel said. "He might want to sleep late." She tried to stop her sister, but Violet was already out the door.

Mabel lay on Violet's polka-dotted bed.

She closed her eyes, trying to think again. A few minutes later, she drifted off to sleep.

When Mabel went downstairs half an hour later, Violet and Uncle Vartan were in the kitchen together.

Uncle Vartan was wearing a green seersucker suit and the same white shirt with silver cuff links. His shoes were shiny green leather. He was humming a tune under his breath.

"We're making pancakes," Violet announced. "Uncle Vartan is teaching me."

"First you mix," Uncle Vartan said, whirling half-a-dozen ingredients rapidly together in a stainless-steel bowl.

"Then you pour . . ." He poured the batter into a hot frying pan and waited a moment. The pancake sizzled. "And finally, you flip. . . ."

He picked up a metal spatula. The pancake sailed up, almost to the ceiling. And then it floated, batter side down, into the pan again.

"Where did you learn to do *that*, Uncle Vartan?" Mabel gasped.

"Nothing to it," he said, winking at Violet. He flipped the pancake again and it landed on a clean plate. He put it in the oven to keep warm. Then he turned to Violet.

"Would you like to make the next one?"

Violet poured batter into the pan. She waited for it to sizzle and then picked up the spatula. "Like this, Uncle Vartan?"

"Give it some wrist," he encouraged.

Violet flipped the pancake. It rose three or four feet in the air, then came down.

"*Very* good, Violet," Uncle Vartan said. "Mabel, would you like a turn?"

Mabel carefully measured batter into the pan. Then Uncle Vartan handed her the spatula.

This will be easy, Mabel thought. *If Violet can do it, I can.*

She slid the spatula under the pancake. To her dismay, the pancake oozed right off and collapsed in the pan.

She looked anxiously at Uncle Vartan. Was he going to laugh at her? Or compare her to her sister?

Uncle Vartan stayed cool. "Don't worry, it'll still be delicious," he said. "Let's try again. This time we'll do it together."

The next pancake soared into the air. But as soon as Uncle Vartan let go of Mabel's wrist, it plummeted downward. *Splat!* Another mess.

Uncle Vartan calmly put it in the oven

with the others. "It takes time and practice," he said.

Which made Mabel wonder: How come Violet did it so well?

It was irritating that her little sister had so much more pancake-making skill than she did. Wasn't it supposed to be the other way around?

The pancakes were delicious. And they kept on coming.

"Are you a chef?" Mabel asked him. "If you are, I want to eat at your restaurant."

She hoped that Uncle Vartan would stay a *very* long time. He was fun. He was kind. He was even nicer than Aunt Dolores.

"Me, too," Violet said.

For once, the two sisters were in total agreement.

Uncle Vartan smiled and sent another pancake spinning high into the air.

Chapter Eleven

After breakfast, Mabel followed Uncle Vartan upstairs to his room.

A delightful fragrance wafted through the air. Mabel sniffed. "What is it?" she asked.

"Bubble bath," Uncle Vartan said. "I take one every morning. Today I had spearmint and orange. Very energizing."

He opened his closet door and took out a pale green tie. Mabel just had time to see dozens of seersucker suits in colors ranging from pale yellow to deepest purple.

How had he fit them into one medium-size leather satchel?

She hoped that all the clothes in his closet meant a *very* long visit.

Uncle Vartan sat down on the bed. He indicated a chair. "Have a seat," he said. He crossed his legs, and Mabel saw stars on his socks. *Cool*, she thought.

"What do you want to talk about?" he asked. "Is something on your mind?"

Now what did she say?

"Uh . . . Uncle Vartan . . ." she said. "I, um, I want to say . . . I'm sorry . . ."

"For what?" He crossed his legs again. This time, she saw purple polka dots on the socks.

She rubbed her eyes. "For, uh, you know . . . I never wrote thank-you notes. You know, for the presents . . ."

"Did you like them?"

"I loved them!" Mabel said. She couldn't take her eyes off his feet. Now she saw a brief flash of a half-moon at his ankle. "So did Violet."

He smiled. His socks had glowing suns. What was going on?

"You're a very good girl, Mabel. Your parents must be proud of you."

"Um, yes. I hope so." Was she having a brain malfunction? Her head was spinning.

"What's happening?" she cried.

"You'll have to ask your mother."

About the *socks*? Or everything else? The mysteries were piling up. Mabel could hardly think straight anymore.

Uncle Vartan stood up. "I'm so glad we had this little talk. Let's go downstairs. I could use a cup of coffee."

Uncle Vartan spread a cloth napkin on his lap and reached for the coffee pot.

He poured himself a cup of black coffee, measured five teaspoons of sugar, and stirred. Then he stacked several donuts on his plate.

Mabel's mother watched him. "You know, Vartan, if I had known you were coming, I would have gone shopping. There's practically nothing left in the refrigerator." She frowned at him. "But today I'm home with the girls. I hate to spend the day at the store with them."

"I can watch them while you shop," Uncle Vartan offered.

"*Yes!*" Mabel and Violet cried in unison.

"I wouldn't dream of imposing on you," their mother said to Uncle Vartan.

"Oh, not at all. I want to spend time with them. Who knows when I'll have another chance?" Uncle Vartan stirred his coffee again and added yet another spoonful of sugar.

"The other thing is that school starts in four days," her mother said. "We need to get organized. . . ."

"Mom," Mabel began. She knew she'd been reminding her mother of this very fact for days. But why did her mother have to bring it up *now*?

Mabel's father came to the rescue. "School preparations can wait," he said. "The girls need to know their uncle. His visit is important."

"It's *way* too important," their mother muttered. She bit her lip.

"Come on, Sandra," her husband said. "Be reasonable."

"Reasonable?" She laughed. "If you only knew . . ."

What is the problem? Mabel wondered. *If we only knew* what.

Was there a family inheritance that favored Uncle Vartan and left her mother out? A great-grandfather locked in an attic? Stolen diamonds?

"They'll be safe with me," Uncle Vartan reassured her parents. The rings on his fingers gleamed. A large sapphire caught the light.

"Safe?" Mabel's mother frowned. "Of course they'll be safe with you. I'm not talking about safety."

"Then what is it, Sandra?" her husband asked.

She didn't answer.

Their father glanced at the clock. "It's time for me to get going." He picked up his laptop and stood up. "I hope you girls have a good time with your uncle Vartan."

"Does that mean . . . ?" Mabel asked.

Her father nodded. "Okay, Sandra?"

Their mother sighed deeply. Then she got up from the table. "I do need to get groceries." She looked at her brother. "I'll be back in a couple of hours. Don't get them in any trouble, Vartan."

"Wouldn't dream of it," Uncle Vartan promised.

Mabel stared at Uncle Vartan's rings. She could have sworn that the sapphire ring had been on the opposite hand just a moment ago.

Chapter Twelve

Mabel wondered if she was the only one who noticed odd things about Uncle Vartan.

Or did everyone else notice, too? Why weren't they saying anything?

Right now, nothing odd was happening. Mabel, Violet, and Uncle Vartan were in the backyard playing Frisbee. It was all totally normal.

As they stood on the lawn, tossing the Frisbee back and forth, Mabel wondered why Uncle Vartan hadn't changed his green leather shoes. With all the clothes in his closet, he probably had a pair of sneakers somewhere.

"I like to play Frisbee in these shoes," Uncle Vartan explained.

"You do?"

"They're greener than grass," Violet said. "The grass likes them."

Count on Violet to say something ridiculous. Mabel threw the Frisbee to her little sister just to shut her up.

"Got it!" Violet yelled.

Mabel blushed. "Don't brag, Violet."

She hoped that Uncle Vartan didn't think *she* was like that.

Uncle Vartan knelt down to pet several

cats who had wandered into the yard. They purred loudly at him.

"Catch this, Mabel!" Violet threw the Frisbee as hard as she could. It wobbled for a moment, then flew straight at a plate-glass window.

"Oh no!" Mabel cried. She ran toward the Frisbee. "Stop!"

At her command, the Frisbee seemed to hesitate. It came to a full stop, changed direction, and flew toward Mabel.

Mabel jumped, reached out, and caught it. Then she stared at the Frisbee as if she

couldn't quite believe what had just happened.

Had she just ordered it not to crash into the window? Had it just obeyed her? But that was crazy! And, anyway, how had she done it?

"Well, well, well," Uncle Vartan said, straightening up and smiling at Mabel. "No one's thrown me a Frisbee yet."

"Here you go," Mabel said.

Uncle Vartan caught the Frisbee on the tip of a finger. His green leather shoes gleamed in the sunshine. The cats' tails waved.

"Throw it to me, Uncle Vartan!" Violet said.

The Frisbee seemed to float through the air. Violet tried to catch it on the tip of her finger like Uncle Vartan, but it fell into the grass.

The cats pounced on it.

A car pulled into the driveway. "That would be your mother," Uncle Vartan said.

He brushed off his hands. "I'm sorry, but I have to go now."

"So soon?" Mabel asked. She glanced in Violet's direction.

Mabel hoped that her little sister would make a scene. Most people found it hard to say no to Violet when she cried and pouted. But Violet didn't throw a tantrum. She wasn't even listening to Uncle Vartan.

"Kitty, kitty," she said. "Here, kitty, kitty."

Uncle Vartan blew Mabel a kiss. "Good-bye," he said. "Take good care of Violet."

"What . . ." Mabel started to say. Was Uncle Vartan leaving on an errand or was he leaving for good?

Before she could finish her sentence, he snapped his fingers and disappeared.

Mabel stared at the place where Uncle Vartan had stood a moment ago. He hadn't left anything behind — not even a trampled blade of grass.

Chapter Thirteen

Mabel walked slowly downstairs from the guest room. It was empty, as if Uncle Vartan had never been there. He hadn't left a single seersucker suit or pair of matching leather shoes. His rings were gone, too, and his leather satchel.

Even the smell of bubble bath had gone.

When and how had he taken them away?

"Uncle Vartan is gone," Mabel told her mother, who was bringing shopping bags into the kitchen.

He vanished into thin air, she wanted to say. Could someone really do that?

"Isn't that just like Vartan?" her mother

said. She put a bag of groceries on the kitchen counter. "Is he coming back?"

"Um," Mabel said, "I don't think so."

"After I did all that shopping, too." Her mother sighed. She didn't seem very upset. In fact, she seemed relieved that her baby brother was gone.

"Do you think he'll come back?" Mabel asked.

"Here one minute, gone the next." Her mother started to put away the groceries. "That's Vartan for you."

"He disappears a lot?" Mabel asked carefully.

"All the time," her mother said. "You can't believe how often he got me in trouble when we were kids. Babysitting for him was a nightmare!"

"I can imagine," Mabel said. She put a box of cereal in the cupboard. "So he just vanished? *Poof!* Like that?"

Her mother suddenly stopped. "What are you talking about, Mabel?"

"You know . . ."

Her mother wouldn't meet her eyes.

"Mom?" Mabel said. "He vanished into thin air a few minutes ago. And he did other stuff."

Her mother opened the refrigerator to put away gallons of juice and milk.

"How come you never talk about Uncle Vartan?" Mabel asked. "How come I didn't know he was your baby brother? Why isn't his picture in any of our photo albums?"

"It's complicated," her mother muttered. She began tossing packages of vegetables into the crisper bin.

"What is it about Uncle Vartan, Mom?" When her mother didn't answer, Mabel said, "Why won't you tell me?"

"Oh dear." Her mother looked ready to cry.

"Please," she urged.

"Magic," her mother said in a low voice. "Vartan has magic."

"Magic," Mabel repeated.

"Vartan has had it since he was very young. It's never been anything but a nuisance for our family. I don't know what he can do, and I don't want to ask."

"So we have magic in the family," Mabel said again. "I knew it!" It was exciting. But it was shocking, too.

"Dolores and I don't have it, thank goodness," her mother said. "But it's in the genes. It appears in early childhood, on a special occasion. Like a birthday or with school starting or a long trip."

"Like, *I* could be magic?" Mabel asked hopefully.

Her mother shuddered. "You don't want magic. It's horrible. Believe me, Vartan ruined my childhood."

"Or Violet?"

"No, please!" Her mother held up a hand. "I sincerely hope that neither you nor Violet ever has magic. We're trying to have a normal life around here."

"But Uncle Vartan . . ."

"It's just like Vartan to waltz in and stir up trouble. That's what he's always done, and that's what he'll always do."

"Does Dad know?"

"Not really." For the first time, her mother looked a little embarrassed. "He knows that Vartan and I don't get along, but I haven't told him every little detail. You know, the magic part."

"But don't you think Dad should know?" Mabel cried. "I mean, having magic in the family is a big deal. . . ."

She still could hardly believe it. And she couldn't believe that her mother had kept it a secret for so long.

"No, I *don't* think your father should know. And don't you ever tell him!" her mother said. "Promise me you won't."

"I promise," Mabel said reluctantly.

"You know my biggest secret now. Don't tell anyone, don't talk about it, and above all, don't ask any more questions. I know you're mature enough to understand this. I don't want to discuss the *M* word ever again. It's way too unpleasant."

Her mother picked up a box of cereal and shoved it into the cupboard. "Oh, and one last thing, Mabel," she said. "If your little sister asks you about magic, don't tell her *anything*."

Chapter Fourteen

One simple word, with only five ordinary letters, explained every confusing, befuddling, and extraordinary event of the last few days.

The rings switching fingers. *Magic.*

The fascinating socks. *Magic.*

The wallet in the freezer. *Magic.*

The vanishing reflection. *Magic.*

The untying shoelaces. *Magic.*

The pancakes flipping four feet high. *Magic.*

The Frisbee turning in midair. *Magic.*

The pepperoni pizza. *Maybe magic.*

Uncle Vartan's disappearing act. *Definitely magic.*

✳   ✳   ✳

That same simple word even explained her mother's mysterious conversation with Aunt Dolores. And Uncle Vartan's visit.

After ten years' absence, why had he suddenly decided to visit? *Magic*.

It was finally clear to Mabel. Now, at the start of a new school year, someone's magic was about to appear.

She thought it might be hers. After all, she had stopped a Frisbee from crashing into a plate-glass window. She had probably untied her own shoelaces, too.

She was the only one who noticed Uncle Vartan's magic — aside from her mother, who had known about it her entire life.

Though she didn't know *why* she had turned a cheese pizza into pepperoni. It was probably just inexperience.

Mabel lay back on her bed and closed her eyes. What would her magic do next? What if she suddenly floated up to her ceiling?

She had always secretly wanted to do this.

But what if someone saw her? Like Dad, who didn't know about the magic. The shock would be too much for him.

Luckily, he was at work now, but Mabel would have to be very careful.

It was a good thing that she was getting the magic. She would use it responsibly. She would make sure that no one was upset by it.

She would keep her mother's secret — even though she wished she didn't have to.

Mabel wondered if Uncle Vartan had left any hints as to how she should manage her magic.

An instruction booklet might have been nice.

Or a rule book. Or even a book of spells.

Maybe there was a 1-800 number she could call to ask questions.

She hoped that her magic wouldn't get

in the way of her winning the Most Helpful Student Award in third grade.

Simone would be so jealous. Mabel would have to break it to her gently. She'd have to swear her to secrecy first, of course.

She only wished she could tell her father! She had never kept secrets from him before. It made her feel sad.

Mabel stood up. She'd better search the house now to see if Uncle Vartan had left any information behind.

Suddenly she knew where it was. It was probably tucked into the fairy-tale book he had sent her and Violet. Maybe that's why he had sent them the book right before his unannounced visit.

Mabel knocked on Violet's door. There was no answer. She pushed the door open.

Something strange was happening in there.

Uncle Vartan's fairy-tale book was flying through the air.

Violet sat cross-legged on the floor. She was practically holding her breath from excitement.

The book zigzagged across the room. It bumped into furniture and knocked toys off their shelves.

"*Violet!*" Mabel cried. "What did I tell you about taking care of books?"

"I didn't bend the pages," Violet protested. The book plummeted into her lap and lay still.

She held up her hands. "They're clean. I washed them first."

"Let me see that book," Mabel snapped. She didn't want to think about what she had just seen it do. Or what it meant.

Mabel sat down on the bed and examined the fairy-tale book. Apart from a small dent on the cover, it was still in mostly good condition.

Out of curiosity, Mabel pointed at

the book and mumbled a few words. The book didn't move.

"I thought so," she said under her breath.

She thought of all the wonderful things she could have done with magic. Like turning pepperoni pizzas into plain ones. Or sharpening all the pencils in the school at once. Or even, when no one was watching, flying around the neighborhood.

But she didn't have the magic. Violet did.

It was Violet.

It had been Violet all along.

That was why the pizza was pepperoni — Violet's favorite.

That was why she could flip pancakes like a pro on her first try.

That was why she had found the wallet in the freezer.

Mabel hadn't stopped the Frisbee. It had been Uncle Vartan, of course. Or maybe even Violet.

Now Violet jumped up. "Will you read me another chapter, Mabel?"

"If you sit quietly, don't ask too many questions, and don't touch the book."

Mabel took a deep breath.

Her unpredictable, messy, rule-breaking, fun-loving, friend-stealing, wallet-finding, crazy little sister had the magic.

Oh boy, was Mabel in trouble now.

About the Author

Anne Mazer is a Mabel who secretly wants to be a Violet. She grew up in a family of writers in upstate New York. She is the author of more than thirty-five books for young readers, including the Scholastic series The Amazing Days of Abby Hayes and the picture book *The Salamander Room*. Visit Anne's Web site at www.AmazingMazer.com.

Coming soon . . .

Sister Magic

Violet Makes a Splash

Chapter One

"We have serious work to do here, Violet," Mabel said. She scratched a mosquito bite on her arm, then picked up a pen.

"Okay, Mabel," said her little sister.

In the living room, clothes and appliances spilled out of boxes and bags. The girls were getting ready for the annual garage sale.

At the end of every summer, the entire neighborhood banded together to hold a giant garage sale. There were fourteen families. Everyone had a table.

Afterward, they had a party. There was delicious food and a pie-baking contest.

While the grown-ups ate, the neighborhood kids played games in the street.

It was one of Mabel's favorite nights of the year.

This year, Mabel was in charge of her family's garage sale table. She was ready.

She glanced at her list. "Today we have to sort through old clothes, winter boots, kitchen utensils, baby toys, books, and other items."

It was a big job, but Mabel could do it.

"Here's the plan. You hand me clothes," Mabel instructed her sister. "I fold and price them. Okay?"

"Okay," Violet agreed. She brought over a couple of baby sweaters. Then she wandered away.

"What are you doing, Violet?"

"Nothing." Violet pulled out a battered cape and ran her fingers over the purple fabric. "I like this," she said.

"It's a piece of old junk," Mabel said.

"No, it isn't." Violet draped the cape over her shoulders and studied her reflection in the mirror.

Mabel folded a little striped sweater and slapped a price tag on it. Then she folded a pale yellow one. "I'm done with the baby sweaters, Violet. Bring me something else to price."

But Violet wasn't listening.

"Violet?" Mabel frowned. "We're not going to get any work done like this."

Her little sister pranced and twirled around the living room. The purple cape billowed out behind her. She hummed a tune.

"Oh, never mind. I'll do it myself," Mabel grumbled.

Yesterday Mabel had said Violet could be her assistant. Now she wished that she had never made the offer.

She wished she had told Violet to find a play date instead.

Five-year-old Violet was nothing but trouble.

She was mischievous and quirky, and she always insisted on having her own way.

She didn't follow instructions; she wasn't reliable. Her face was always smudged. Her hair was always wild. Her clothes never matched.

Mabel, on the other hand, wore coordinated outfits, even in the summer. Her hair was always combed. Her face was always washed.

She was neat, organized, trustworthy, and helpful. She was eight years old and mature beyond her age.

Her mother thought that organizing a garage sale was too much work for an eight and a five year old.

She was probably right about the five year old. But Mabel knew she could do it. With or without Violet.

She would show everyone. Mabel was going to have the best garage sale, *ever*.

Before she started work, Mabel made a list of things to do:

1. Sort books by title and subject.
2. Fold used clothing in piles according to color and size.
3. Hang up skirts, dresses, and coats.
4. Organize baby toys in bins.
5. Separate children's clothing into categories: "infant," "toddler," and "young child."
6. Price everything with color-coded tags.

Mabel loved being in charge and running the show.

She loved doing things well.

She loved having people say, "I knew I could count on you, Mabel."

As Mabel worked, Violet climbed onto the couch and jumped off. The purple cape flew out behind her. Then she climbed back up and jumped again.

Mabel was still pricing when she heard the crash. She dropped everything and ran to her sister.

Violet had tripped over a box of wire hangers, banged into a small lamp, and fallen in the middle of some shopping bags.

"Are you all right?" Mabel cried.

Violet nodded. Things were scattered all around her. Her cape was twisted and torn. A hanger was caught on her foot.

She stood up slowly and brushed herself off.

"This is more of a mess than ever." Mabel tried to be patient. "If you're not going to help, could you at least stay out of the way?"

"Sorry, Mabel."

Mabel picked up a pair of lime green tights with only a tiny hole in the toe and wrote a price tag for them.

Violet climbed onto the couch again. "Watch me fly!"

"Did you hear what I just said?" Mabel felt exasperated. How many times did she have to repeat herself? "Stay out of my way! I'm busy!"

It was hopeless, she thought. Why had she ever thought of asking Violet to help? Violet made everything a hundred times more difficult.

A wind gusted across the room. Where was her troublemaking little sister now?

Then Mabel heard a giggle. It came from right above her head.

She looked up.

Violet was floating near the ceiling.

The purple cape swayed lightly in the breeze. Wire hangers hung from Violet's

arms like bracelets. Violet's dirty bare feet dangled above Mabel's nose.

Mabel's heart began to pound. Her sister could do *this*? She could *fly*?

Mabel and Violet are in over their heads!

Sister Magic
Violet Makes a Splash

BY ANNE MAZER
ILLUSTRATIONS BY BILL BROWN
📖 SCHOLASTIC

When Violet uses her new powers to conjure up a swimming pool, things get complicated. What will the neighbors think? And how will she and Mabel ever explain this to their parents?

📖 SCHOLASTIC
www.scholastic.com

SISMAG2